Wife Next Door

Wife Next Door

A WIFE-TO-BE NOVELLA
A'NDREA J. WILSON

Divine Garden Press

Published by Divine Garden Press, LLC
P.O. Box 371
Soperton, GA 30457
www.divinegardenpress.com

ISBN-13: 978-0692324776
ISBN-10: 0692324771

Cover Design & Interior Layout by Divine Lit Services
www.divinelit.com

Above all, love each other deeply, because love covers over a multitude of sins.

(1 Peter 4:8, NIV)

The Most Beautiful Girl in the World

Morris

I'm in love with her. I always have been. It's so hard to watch her embrace another man when I know it should be me making her happy. If only things were different, I would have laid my claim to her a long time ago. Right now, she would be Mrs. Felicia Bryson instead of that knucklehead Corey Dillard's girlfriend. That jerk doesn't deserve a dog much less a beautiful and loving woman like my childhood best friend, Felicia.

Corey and Felicia are in the driveway of her parents' home. Felicia is sitting on the hood of Corey's Lexus sedan, while he stands between her knees, attempting to get much closer. Every couple of minutes, she giggles and pushes him away. It's just like her to play the coy role. I wish more women still had that attribute.

I watch their banter from the window of my bedroom. It's amazing all of the things I have seen from my second floor view. I've practically watched all of Felicia's adolescent years from up here. I'm surprised that by now she hasn't figured out that I can see her. I'm not stalking her or anything like that. I just like to make sure she's safe. As long as I'm around, no one, including Cory Dillard, is going to hurt her.

I remember the day her parents moved into the house next door, twenty-six years ago with a large moving truck full of fancy furniture and a Mercedes Benz that caused our neighbors to ooh and ahh. See, in a small town, everything is all mixed up and mashed together—black and white, rich and poor, city people and country folks. Her parents have money, a lot of money, but that didn't change the fact that they moved into the house next door to my parents who are infamous for robbing Peter just to pay Paul.

Felicia was 9 when she moved here; I was 10. Now we're 35 and 36 respectively. In addition to forming a close friendship over the years, we made a pact when she was 16 that if by the time she turned 35, she wasn't married, I would make her my bride. It all seemed inconsequential back then, some would even say childish, but I've never forgotten that pledge I made to her. Matter-of-fact, today is her 35th birthday. But it's more than just her birthday. It's the day I'm going to ask her to marry me.

I stare out the window at Felicia and Corey Dillard. Eventually, he will leave, and when he does, I'll make my move.

Felicia

I hate living with my parents, especially in the rural South. It's my 35th birthday, and when I blow out the candles on my cake later today, my wish will be to get out of here—out of this house, hopefully even out of this town. If I'd known when my family moved to Sweet Lake, Georgia twenty-something years ago that we would indefinitely get stuck here, I would have begged my parents not to leave Boston, my true hometown. My parents were doing well up north, owned a few fast food franchise restaurants. Then my mother, Belinda, was diagnosed with heart disease, and my father, Vincent, decided he'd rather lose Boston and his money-making businesses than his wife. He sold the restaurants and our three-story brick house and moved us to his hometown, Sweet Lake. He'd inherited a house and eight acres of land from my grandparents several years prior. Concerned for my mother's health and hoping the fresh, country air would save her life, my dad relocated Mom, me, and my older sister, Stacy, to a small town near the coast of Georgia. Notwithstanding my disapproval, he was right—the move did save her life.

When it came to moving to Sweet Lake, culture shock describes my experience at best. The abrupt change in scenery and pace almost crushed my childhood. If it weren't for my next door neighbor, Morris, I think I might have lost my mind and ran away. The girls didn't like me and Stacy because we were too citified, but the boys couldn't get enough of us, tired of the lame chicks they'd known since preschool. Of course, our "fresh meat" status wore off after a year or two, but despite the boys backing up—just a little—the girls never stepped forward. We became permanent outsiders amongst the girls, which was fine with us. For the most part, we kept to ourselves and plotted to leave Sweet Lake the minute we wrapped our manicured fingers around our high school diplomas.

Growing up, Stacy always had a boyfriend. During our teen years, she was barely around. If she wasn't working at the new fast food restaurant my daddy opened in Sweet Lake, she was out gallivanting with some boy. She is three years older than me, and when she graduated from Sweet Lake High and jetted back to Boston for college and to reclaim her former life, I was left to endure three more years of back country road thinking by myself. Thankfully, Morris was a great friend and confidant who looked out for me during those years, not allowing anyone to mistreat me.

During high school, Morris was my everything. He was my study partner, my date to the senior prom, and my first kiss. We even came up with this stupid idea that if we weren't married by 35, we'd marry each other. Morris is older than me by a year, but he graduated from high school the same year as I did because his illness caused him to miss a lot of school when he was in elementary. Morris has sickle cell anemia, a blood disease that is prevalent among African Americans. I think being sick made him more empathetic toward others, even as a child. With both of our families dealing with the chronic illness of one of our members, we all seemed to bond and take care of each other. Holidays, special occasions, and Sunday dinners brought us all together as if we were extended family. There were innumerous trips back and forth between the few acres that separated our dwellings to borrow sugar or just say hello. It only made sense that Morris and I would become so tightly knit.

A part of me felt bad for him. He was a great guy—a cutie if I say so myself—but his condition was a constant barrier, keeping him from spreading his wings and flying away from the nest. Once we graduated, I went back to Boston like Stacy for college, but Morris stayed local, taking classes at a community college and working for my father as a shift manager. While I was away, we kept in contact by phone, emails, and the thoughtful care packages he would send me every semester. I'd get to see him every Thanksgiving and Christmas, but during the summers, I usually took on a temporary job in

Massachusetts and wouldn't get a chance to come home. A couple of times, he surprised me and showed up at my dorm, visiting me for a long weekend and reminding me how much I missed being around him. Once I finished my Bachelor's degree, I decided to remain in Boston, becoming roommates with Stacy and starting a full-time position in advertising for a snack food company. Stacy and I as roomies lasted nine years, until Stacy got married to a pediatrician, Lewis Strong. Without a thought, Stacy dumped me and our family last name, Jefferson, and was whisked away to her suburban lifestyle—and eventually two children. As much as I was happy for my sister, I was left to pay the rent for our two bedroom apartment, which was too pricey for my meager salary. Six months later when the lease ended, I packed my bags and moved to a more affordable side of town, into a studio apartment that was half the cost. For the next three years, all was decent in my life—not well but not bad either. I had a steady job, plenty of friends, and even a beautiful man to woo me from time to time. But then the bottom fell out. The company I worked for got bought out by a bigger company and pink slips were handed out like Halloween candy. Unfortunately, I got the axe. Severance pay and unemployment kept me for several months, but of course, my bills exceeded the amount I was getting, and after struggling unsuccessfully to find an acceptable job, I gave up and moved back home to Sweet Lake. My father immediately made me the director of adverting and sales for the now five restaurants he owns—a position he created specifically for yours truly.

I have to admit, the first few months of living in my parents' house again were a huge relief. After being so stressed out about keeping a roof over my head, it was bliss to no longer worry about food, rent, electricity, and every other bill that had been haunting me. But now, the experience has become bittersweet. I enjoy being near my parents and Morris, but I feel so caged in. The town is so small and everyone is simpleminded. No one tries anything new or thinks outside of the box. I have to travel thirty minutes to Savannah just to get a little culture or shop at a mall that has more than twenty stores.

I almost forgot about Corey. How could I ever forget about him? He makes living in Sweet Lake bearable, and honestly, he's the only reason I'm not working on a plan to move up north again. We've been dating for two years and I can't help but wonder if he is ever going to pop the question. We've talked about marriage a couple of times, but Corey is old school—you know, wants to have all of his ducks in a row before he jumps the broom. I respect his desire to be able to take care of me, so I'm laying off him and going to give him another year to get himself together. But I swear, if he doesn't propose to me by my birthday next year, I'm out of here! I love Corey and I want to be with him, but I refuse to waste the rest of my 30's on a man who may never be ready for the next step. The only way I'm staying anywhere near Sweet Lake is if I'm married to a man I really love.

Corey is standing in front of me, talking slick. I don't know why these country men think they can get one over on a city girl. Nothing he is saying to me right now is anything new. I've heard all of the lines before, and they've never worked—not in the past and definitely not now. Like my mother always told me and Stacy, "Why buy the cow when you can get the milk for free?" My sister didn't give away free milk and she's a purchased cow—not to call her a farm animal, but I'm just saying. If Corey wants any milk from me, he will have to pay the cost and marry me. I laugh at his antics and slide down off his car, rejecting his offer to give me a birthday I'll never forget. Corey's not used to a woman playing hard to get. He lives in the next city over, Springtown, and is the only orthodontist in a twenty mile radius. He makes plenty of money, so I don't understand what more he needs to "get together financially" in order to marry me. Sounds like a copout if you ask me. My momma didn't raise a fool, so as much as I love this man, I remain true to my values.

"Thanks for the birthday present," I say to him, swinging the small gift bag in his direction. He bought me earrings—my birthstone, not a diamond, and not a ring. I can't help but feel a tad disappointed that I haven't gotten what I really want from him, but I suck up my feelings and appreciate the thought behind the gift.

"No problem," he says. "Are you sure you don't want to . . ."

"I'm sure," I say. "My parents are making me dinner with a cake tonight. Sort of a family tradition when I'm home. So, I'll see you tomorrow?"

"I've got patients all day, but we'll do something this weekend, okay?"

"Sure. Thanks again," I say before giving him a kiss on the cheek and backing away from his Lexus. He jogs around to the driver side, gets in, and pulls off, waving in the process. I'm about to head into the house when I hear the grass ruffling not far away. I look up and see Morris walking in my direction with a small gift bag in his hand. Another present. Don't you just love birthdays?

Thirty-Five Candles

Morris

I know Felicia so well that when I saw the hint of an unimpressed look spread across her face, I knew it was time to leave the obscurity of my bedroom and head over to her house to save her from Corey Dillard. To my appreciation, he was peeling off in his car by the time I got halfway across her parents' lawn. Corey didn't care much for me, and the feeling was mutual. I tried to avoid him for the most part, but when I felt it was necessary, I didn't think twice about showing up out of the blue and busting up his weak game. As far as I was concerned, he was a loser. I just wish that Felicia could see that he wasn't worth her time.

Felicia smiles brightly when she sees me coming and waits on the porch for my approach. Although her smile quiets my rapidly beating heart, the nervousness I am feeling refuses to go away. *Can I really do it? Can I really propose to her? Will she reject me? Will she look at me like I'm crazy? Will this ploy for her heart ruin our friendship?* The endless questions consume my mind as I move closer and closer to her.

I've been plotting out this day for two months. After my last sickle cell crisis, my doctor sat me down and had a heart-to-heart with me.

"Morris, I'm going to be straight with you," Dr. Finley said. "You've been having these crises more frequently. Your sickled cells are blocking oxygen from getting to your organs and there's quite a bit of damage to your liver and kidneys. On average, people with this disorder live into their 40's, some longer, but with your health declining . . . You're thirty-six, right?"

"Yeah," I said quietly.

"Is there anything that you really want to do in your lifetime? Any goals or dreams that you haven't fulfilled yet?"

I'd actually been thinking about my dreams a lot. Chronic pain makes you realize what's truly important. "I guess I'd like to get married, have a family. You know, leave a legacy behind."

"Well, I suggest you get working on that soon. With your condition, there are no guarantees. We're doing everything we can to help you fight anemia, but you have to make the best of each and every day. You understand?"

I knew what he was trying to say. He didn't have to say the words. "Yeah, I understand."

That was two months ago. Now, I'm walking up the porch steps, nearing the woman of my dreams, carrying an engagement ring inside a purple gift bag, and following the doctor's orders. He suggested that I pursue my dreams, and that is what I intend to do.

Felicia

"What's in the bag?" I ask Morris once he's standing directly in front of me.

He grins. "It's for me to know and you to find out."

I huff. I know the gift is for me, so he should just fork it over and stop playing games. "Are you going to give it to me or what?"

He must be amused because he laughs. "Aren't we inpatient? Yes, I'm going to give it to you . . . after I get a piece of that birthday cake."

Typical Morris. He's looking to be repaid for his generosity . . . in cake. "How do you even know there's a cake?" I ask, testing him.

He puts the gift bag behind his back as if to tell me he's not willing to negotiate or up for excuses. "With your momma, there's always a cake. The question isn't is there a cake, it's what time are you cutting it?"

I sigh and reach for the screen door's handle. "Well, since you're withholding my present ransom over a piece of cake, we'll have to speed up the cake cutting process. Come on in," I say as I pull the screen door open and walk into the house. Morris follows me inside and we enter the kitchen where my mom already has dinner cooked. I peep into the dining room to see my homemade birthday cake on display in the middle of the long, oak table. My mom and Morris exchange pleasantries while I sneak into the dining room and carefully swipe the side of the cake with my index finger, coating it with lemon frosting. Licking my finger, I enjoy an immediate sugar rush, savoring the sweet flavor.

"So, you're not even going to wash your hands before putting your fingers all over the cake?" Morris says, catching me in the act. "Nasty."

I lick the last bit of frosting off my finger and say, "If you don't like it, you don't have to eat any. Just be sure to hand over the gift, will ya?"

He shakes his head defiantly. "No, I will not. I want some of that cake, even if you have tainted it with your grubby paws."

"How do you know my hands are dirty?"

"Because you were just sitting on top of Corey Dillard's car with your hands all over him. The guy's trash so I know your hands aren't clean."

I twist my lips. Morris always seems to know everything—at least everything about me. "Spying on me again, I see. My hands were not all over him, it was the opposite way around. And furthermore he's not trash, he's my boyfriend. Why do you always refer to him by his full name?"

He sighs as if he is bored. "First name only privilege is reserved for people I like. Keep working my nerves and you'll become Felicia Jefferson."

"Whatever, Morris Bryson. Why don't we both go and wash our hands so that we can eat dinner."

An hour and a half later, Morris and I have finished dinner and dessert with my parents, and are now in my bedroom, lounging on my bed, watching reruns of *The George Lopez Show*. Every few minutes, I eye the purple gift bag, wondering why he's being so secretive about his gift, and why he just won't give it to me. Usually, he can't wait for me to open his presents. His refusal to hand over the gift increases my anticipation about it. After the third commercial break, I can't take it any longer.

"Okay, you've had your cake. Either give me that gift bag or get out of my house," I say with a serious expression, but holding back a smile.

He shakes his head. "Uh, last time I checked, this was your parents' house. Mrs. Jefferson said I can stay as long as I want."

"Morris!" I plead.

"Okay, okay!" He laughs. "Let me get my thoughts together so that I can do this right."

I watch him critically. Why does he have to get his thoughts together? Is there really a right way to give someone a birthday present? His confusing words make me nervous. I hope he doesn't have bad news.

He gets up from the side of the bed he's been lounging on and walks over to my side. He sits down at the edge of the bed next to me, which causes me to sit up straight. He's so serious now—this is all so weird.

"Felicia, I've known you since you were nine. I'll never forget that day when you walked into my life and changed my world. Before then, it was hard for me to connect with people because I didn't want people pitying me because I was sick. But you always treated me like I was normal. You gave me hope."

"Aww," I say, feeling emotionally moved by his confession.

He clears his throat. "Let me finish. I'm going to get this out even if it kills me."

Get what out? I nod to tell him to continue even though I have no idea where he is going with all of this sappy talk.

"I'll also never forget that day we made that pact to get married."

"That was so crazy, wasn't it?" I ask, laughing at the thought. "We were young and silly."

"Yes, it was crazy, and we were young, but it wasn't silly."

He gets down on one knee and I lose my breath. *What in the world is he doing? Is he about to . . .*

"Morris, what are you doing?" I ask frantically, standing up in the process.

"Felicia, please sit back down," he orders, and I comply.

"Felicia, I fell in love with you the first time I saw you. I was a child, but the moment I saw you, I couldn't get you out of my mind. You were always so beautiful and innocent, and I knew that it was my job to watch over you."

"Morris, I don't understand."

"I know this is not what you were expecting me to say. Maybe you don't feel the same. Maybe you don't love me too, but hear me out."

I nod, speechless.

"Today is your thirty-fifth birthday and I intend to keep my promise to you, to marry you."

"Morris, you don't have to—"

"Let me finish." He reaches into the purple gift bag and pulls out a ring box, opening it in the process.

My mouth drops wide open as my eyes fix on the sparkling diamond ring inside the box. It's a round diamond—maybe 2-carats—in a gold solitaire setting. I look up at him in shock. He's proposing to me. Morris, not Corey, is actually proposing to me!

"Felicia Jefferson, will you marry me?"

My words feel caught inside my throat. "Morris, I . . . but we're not . . . I don't . . . I don't know what to say," I finally manage to say.

"I understand. I know that this is unexpected."

I nod and look back down at the diamond. I wish I could take it from him, I would love to be engaged, but it's not right. I can't marry him.

"Yes, it is," I say gently. "You know I love you, but I'm not in love with you, at least I don't think I am. I mean, I have a boyfriend."

"Let me explain," he says. "I know that this is a bit inconvenient with you dating Corey Dillard and all, but there's a reason I'm asking you this right now. Yes, it's your birthday, and yes, we made a pact nineteen years ago, but there's more to the story. Now, I don't want you to feel sorry for me or obligated to me, but it's only fair that I tell you the whole truth. My sickle cell crises are getting worse, more frequent. The pain is . . . well, the disease is really doing a number on my organs. My doctor didn't say the words, but I can tell that he doesn't think I have much longer to live."

"What? No! He's wrong. It's not true," I cry. Before I can stop them, tears begin to pour from my eyes.

He pulls me into his arms and hugs me tightly. "This is why I hesitated telling you this part. I don't want you to cry."

"I can't lose you," I say to him. My heart is pounding and breaking at the same time.

He pulls back from me and softly wipes the tears away from my eyes. "Felicia, one day, you will lose me. That's why I want us to get married. I don't know how much longer I have to live, but I don't want to spend another day away from you. You're my best friend, the very best person I know. Even if I only have a few months left, I want to spend them being happy with you. I know I'm asking for a lot from you, but if this is the last thing I do here on earth, I want you to know how I feel about you, and I want a chance to be as close to you as I possibly can."

I nod. I can't believe this is happening. I always knew he was sick and that he'd probably die before me, but I never thought it would be this soon. Morris is strong, and he's never made a big deal about his condition. I know him well. If he is asking me to marry him because he thinks he's going to die, then his health has really taken a turn for the worst. He wouldn't use the sympathy card on me unless he absolutely had to.

I don't know how I'm going to do this, but I'll have to marry him. I may not be in love with him, but how can I deny his dying request? The thought of it brings fresh tears to my eyes and I breakdown crying. Once again, he embraces me, rubbing me on my back and comforting me. It's a little selfish of me to need the comforting when he's the one knocking on death's door, but I can't seem to contain my emotions.

After several minutes, I glance up at him, sadly. "Okay. I'll marry you," I say, sniffling.

He takes the ring out of the box and slides it on to my ring finger. It fits perfectly, but I'm not surprised. Morris knows everything about me, from the size of my jeans to the size of my ring finger.

"Felicia, thank you for saying yes, but I want you to do me a favor. Think about it—no pray about it overnight. If you want to change your mind tomorrow, I'll understand. If not, let's start planning for the wedding. Since time is limited, I'd like to get married in a month at my father's church. I've been saving up money for a long time, and I've saved more than enough to buy us a house. I've actually already picked it out and paid for it. I'll show it to you tomorrow if you still want to do this. I paid cash for it so once I transition, you'll be able to keep the house. I also have a sizeable life insurance policy, so you'll be well taken care of once I'm gone."

"Stop talking like this!" I say, no longer able to listen to what he's saying.

"I'm sorry, but I need you to know all of this."

"I can't hear anymore. Not now," I say, sobbing.

"Okay. I think I've said enough for now. I'll leave and give you some time alone."

He kisses me on the forehead and leaves my room, closing the door behind him. When I can no longer hear his footsteps in the hallway, I burst into tears again. What am I going to do without my best friend? And even more immediately, how can I marry the man next door?

Playing House

Morris

I feel horrible for the way I left things with Felicia. I didn't want her pity, but it would have been wrong to ask for her hand in marriage without fully disclosing my prognosis and rationale for the sudden request. I know I broke her heart by being so forthcoming about my plans to provide for her in the likelihood of my demise, but in order for her to make an informed decision about this proposal, she needed to know all of my intentions. It took everything within me not to allow myself to be overtaken by tears along with her, but both of us being distraught at the same time would have only made her pain worse—mine too.

I return home in a sullen mood. My parents attempt to greet me, but I wave them away and head for the safety of my bedroom.

"Morris," my father, Michael, calls out for me when I don't respond to their cheerful hellos.

I dare not turn back. I am an inch away from an emotional breakdown, and one word out of my mouth, even a hello, is enough to send me over the edge.

"Morris," my father says, trying again.

"Let him be," I hear my mother, Allison, say to him with concern in her voice.

My father lets out a heavy sigh, but doesn't call out to me again. By this point, I've reached the landing of the second floor and am relieved that my mother has intervened on my behalf. My father, with sixty-plus years of pride, would have followed me upstairs and demanded an explanation had my mom not spoken up. I can't help but wonder if I had more time to live would Felicia have that much influence over me. Probably so. She probably already did.

I make it to my bedroom, shut the door behind me, lumber over to my bed, and allow my body to fall down on it, face down. My mind is racing with my recent conversation with Felicia and her agreement to marry me.

She could always change her mind, I think, but I know she probably won't. I saw the look in her eyes. She is going to do whatever she feels she needs to do to make me happy. Knowing this should bring me joy, but I feel cheated for her, resenting the sacrifice that she will make for me. I went into this proposal fully realizing that she will end up losing. Yes, I plan to be an excellent husband, but she will have to watch me die. What kind of marriage is that?

She'll also have to commit her life to me, someone she doesn't love. She even said so herself. She'll have to give up Corey Dillard, which is the only part of this whole ordeal that I can actually smile about. I wonder how she'll do it, how she'll break-up with him. He'll probably find someone else in a matter of days. He might even try to confront me about stealing his woman. I'm not a fighter, but I wouldn't mind decking him one good time. An unexpected uppercut to the jaw and I bet he'd go down. *Good riddance, Corey Dillard.*

My thoughts shift to the house that I purchased for us. After that life-changing conversation with Dr. Finley, I immediately went house shopping, making my first withdrawal ever from the savings account I have at Sweet Lake Bank. I've lived with my parents my entire life. It's not that I couldn't afford my own place, but with my medical issue, my parents thought it was best that I not live alone. I agreed with them because I saw it as an opportunity to save up some cash to buy a house one day, get married, and whatnot. Working the past dozen or so years as the store manager for Mr. Jefferson's Sweet Lake restaurant, and not having to pay out for living expenses has created a large nest egg for me. Dr. Finley's words to me that day reminded me of why I had tucked away so much money, and why it's important that I use it now to experience my dreams before it's too late.

My parents don't know that I proposed to Felicia. They know I've always had a crush on her, but they don't know that I've finally done something about it. I'll wait to tell them until after I see her tomorrow, after she confirms that she really will go through with the marriage. Thinking about tomorrow makes me anxious. Philippians 4:6 crosses my mind. *Be anxious for nothing, but in everything by prayer and supplication with thanksgiving let your requests be made known to God.* Understanding what I must do, I whisper a prayer to the One above.

"Let Your will be done, and give us both peace."

Felicia

I wake up the day after my birthday with a headache. I'd hoped that a good night of sleep would erase the awful feelings about Morris' declining health and my agreement to marry him, but I find that hasn't happened. The moment I open my eyes, the memories of last night flood my thoughts, bringing me back to a state of pure unhappiness.

I force myself out of bed with the thought of making a cup of hot tea. I throw on my robe and slippers, and make it all of the way into the kitchen before another dose of reality hits me.

I have to break up with Corey.

I groan.

Corey and I don't have a perfect relationship, but I really do care about him and I sincerely hoped that we'd get married one day. I've had many fantasies of my life as his wife and what our children would look like. We'd have this grand wedding and build a six-bedroom house on one of the barrier islands. It is all so right in my dreams, but my reality has thrown me a crushing blow. My dreams of becoming Mrs. Dillard will never be. I'll never marry Corey because I have to marry Morris. The thought of it makes me want to cry.

Morris is a good man—the best man—I'm just not in love with him. I wish I was in love with him because it would be so much easier to give myself to marriage with him if I was. It wouldn't feel like I was a pirate's prisoner getting ready to walk the plank, heading straight for my demise. Not that life with Morris would be bad, but a loveless marriage can't be enjoyable—can it?

I want to continue my pity party, but time is ticking away and Morris doesn't have the kind of time that I do. My best friend needs me right now, and I would never be able to live with myself if he died without having his final wish granted, especially when I'm the only one who can give him what he wants. I swallow my heartache, pick up my cell phone, and make two calls. First, I call Corey and tell him we need to meet for dinner tonight, my treat. I plan to break up with him over barbeque ribs, corn on the cob, and baked beans. It's only right that I pay for our last meal together.

Second, I call Morris. I know he is waiting for me to confirm my decision to marry him, and I refuse to keep him waiting any longer than necessary.

"Hello?" he answers, sounding just as solemn as I feel. I know my best friend's voice, and based on it, I realize that the weight of his proposal is not just heavy on me, it's heavy on him too.

"Hey, Morris," I say. "It's me."

"Hey, Felicia. Did you sleep okay?"

I rub my tired, puffy eyes. I'm scared to look in the mirror because I'm sure that I look like a raccoon. "Honestly, not really."

"I'm sorry. I know it's my fault."

I sigh. It's not his fault that he's dying, nor is it his fault that he wants to take advantage of his final days. Ruining my birthday is his fault, but I'm not angry with him. How could I be? "No need to be sorry. I'm calling to tell you that I'm going to do it. I'm going to marry you like I said I would last night."

"Are you sure?"

"Yes. I know that if the tables were turned, you'd do the same for me."

"You're right," he says. "I would. Thank you, Felicia."

"No problem," I say, but my words aren't true. I do have a problem, but I'll have to get over it.

"Do you want to see the house?" he asks.

There's no point in avoiding the inevitable. "Yeah, let's do that."

"Okay. I'll pick you up in an hour," he says before we end the call.

An hour and fifteen minutes later, we are driving down Bear Creek Road on the outskirts of our town. It's a sunny October morning, and in Coastal Georgia, the weather resembles summer more than autumn. As I ride in Morris' Ford F150 alongside him, I take in the scenery. Pine and pecan trees line up on the roadside like an army about to march out into war. Large oak trees with Spanish moss draping from their branches provide shade from the bright and relentless sun. Plush green grass grows untamed in the places where humans have not laid claim to the land. Squirrels and a turtle run across the road, seemingly unconcerned that they are in the path of speeding cars. As much as I often think about leaving this place, I cannot deny that it's much more enchanting than Boston.

The truck slows and turns into the long driveway of a new looking home. In the country, many homes are older and have history to them, but this house is modern and appears unlived in. This can't be Morris' house—I mean our house. I was expecting something less . . . expensive. I glance over at

Morris who has parked the truck in front of the garage—most rural homes don't have attached garages—and is now grinning in pride.

"Well?" he says.

I feel a bit tongue-tied. "I–Is this . . . the house you bought?"

He glances at the house. "It is. Do you like it?"

"Yes, of course. But how can you afford this?"

"I've been saving for years to buy a beautiful house in the country for my wife. I know your taste. You wouldn't have been comfortable living in an old house," he says, and he's right. My parents have spoiled me and I'm used to having nice things. Morris and his folks live very modestly. I just assumed the house he had purchased would reflect the way he's always lived, not the way I do.

"Did you have this built?" I ask, still shocked by the impressive house. "It looks as if no one has ever lived here."

"It is new, but no, I didn't have it built," he says. "The original owner went bankrupt right after completing the house and the bank foreclosed on it. It's been sitting empty for about two years. The moment I saw this place, I knew you would love it, so I purchased it."

As much as I like—no love—this home, I can't let Morris go into debt trying to please me. "But what about the mortgage? Will it be too much for you?"

He shakes his head, then reaches over and rubs my arm. "You're not listening to me. There is no mortgage. I paid cash for the house. It's ours, free and clear. And when I pass, it will be yours."

I stare at Morris in disbelief. My eyes water at the realization that he has planned all of this out to the letter. He is sure that he is going to die and he has gone out of his way to make my life as comfortable as possible as his wife and soon-to-be widow. *Oh God, help us,* I think.

He grabs my left hand, the one that is now wearing his engagement ring. "I know this is hard for you to hear," he says, "but it has to be said. You'll be taken care of both while I'm alive and after I'm gone. I have enough money for us to enjoy however long I have left, and I also have a large life insurance policy that you'll be the only beneficiary of when my time comes. I know that you're working for your father, but I'd like you to quit so that we can spend as much time as possible together. If you want to go back to work once I . . . I'm okay with you going back to work later, but for now, I would like you to be with me."

I nod. Morris resigned from his job about a month ago, never giving a reason as to why. It all makes sense now. He has been preparing for his retirement and death. The thought brings shivers up and down my spine. I cross my arms in front of my chest and rub my shoulders in an effort to comfort myself.

"Let's take a look at the inside," he says before exiting the truck. I also get out of the vehicle and follow him into the house.

I instantly fall deeper in love with the house. It has six-bedrooms, four and a half bathrooms, a large kitchen with an island, and an even larger family room. The master bedroom has two huge walk-in closets and a bathroom with a double vanity, garden tub, and separate shower. The backyard is massive, enough to put in a pool, start a garden, and build a guest house. There is also a small pond on the property with a gazebo nearby. I now understand why the previous owner went into debt.

"How much did you pay for this place?" I ask Morris as we walk the grounds outside the house.

He glances down at his shoes then back up at me. He always does this when he wants to avoid a question. "I'm not going to tell you, but I can say that I got a really good price for it since they were having a hard time selling it. Based on the market value, I already have quite a bit of equity built up in it. I don't want you to worry about the cost. What good is saving up a bunch of money if you never get to spend it? I've been saving my entire adulthood and now I finally have something to show for it."

He turns and looked at me. "We need to discuss the wedding. We don't have time to create a perfect wedding, but I'm sure we can make it beautiful. The most important thing is having those who love us there. I've reserved my father's church for the first weekend in November. There's a local wedding coordinator who's willing to work within our timeframe. I'll give you her contact information and you can let her know anything special you'd like to include."

I glance around the property again, then say, "Okay. I just have one request."

"Anything."

"Let's have the wedding here, by the pond." The house is beautiful and if I'm going to marry Morris and live here with him, all of our new memories, our final memories, should be here.

He nods. "If that's what you want."

I offer a weak smile. "It's what I want."

"Have you told Corey Dillard?" he asks.

I've been trying not to think about my upcoming conversation with my boyfriend. The most difficult aspect of marrying Morris is letting Corey go. "Not yet. I'm meeting him tonight for dinner. I'll tell him then."

Morris brushes strands of stray hair away from my face. "As much as I don't care for him, I'm sorry for putting you in such an awkward position."

"I know. It'll be okay, it's just going to take some getting used to." I look around the premises again, willing myself to be grateful for my new blessings. "Thank you for the house. I love it."

"Good," he says. "I love you."

I offer him a smile. I can't return his sentiment, not the way he means it. I wonder if I ever will.

Let's Just Kiss and Say Goodbye

Felicia

Corey and I nestle into a booth at a local, award-winning barbeque restaurant. We order our food and sip on sweet tea while we wait for our dinner. In my mind, I replay the words I need to say to him, but every time I think I'm ready to speak them, I lose courage.

I find myself staring at him, taking in the man that I hoped I would marry. He's a little too good looking and a bit overly self-assured, but he's also charming, focused, and supportive. I can't count the times that he's encouraged me to go to graduate school or push forward in my career. He believes in pursuing dreams and overcoming obstacles. Corey's not so bad, even if Morris can't see what I see in him.

"What?" Corey asks, noticing my intense gaze.

"Nothing," I say, blushing and looking away.

"Don't lie to me. You've been acting weird all evening, and now you're staring at me like I'm dead or something. What's up?"

He thinks I'm staring at him like he's dead. What an observation! I feel like he's the one dying instead of Morris. I know the minute I tell him the truth, "I'm marrying Morris," Corey and I, our relationship will die. It's almost like knowing your loved one is brain dead and that you should pull the electricity cord on the ventilator that's keeping them alive, but purposely waiting hours or even days because you just need a little more time before you say goodbye. I don't want to kill us, but Corey and I are over and I must pull the cord. I must let us die.

A tear escapes the corner of my eye and I don't try to hide it. What's the purpose? Heartache isn't meant to be easy.

"Felicia, what's wrong? What's going on?" Corey says, leaning in closer to me.

The waitress interrupts by bringing over our food. I sniffle back my tears and allow her to serve us. Once she leaves our table, I notice that Corey's eyes have not left me. He's still waiting for my response. He has no idea that I am about to end us.

"Felicia?" he pleads.

I'm not wearing my engagement ring. I took it off because I didn't want to tip him off before I was able to explain. I look down at my barren finger and mentally pray to God for the strength to do what I must.

I clear my throat. "Corey, I need to tell you something."

He looks concerned. "What? What's going on? Did something happen?"

"Morris. Morris is dying," I say, my voice a little louder than a whisper.

Corey looks stunned. "What? I mean, I know he's always sick, but he's actually dying?"

I nod. "His doctor believes so."

He reaches across the table and squeezes my hand. "Baby, I'm so sorry. I know he's your friend and this must be really hard for you."

I swallow. "There's more."

His eyes widen. "I'm listening."

I glance down at the table. "He asked me to marry him."

I expect him to get upset and maybe yell out, but instead I hear him let out a chuckle. "Wait. Okay, I'm confused. Let me get this right. Morris is dying, but he asked you to marry him? Are you joking?"

I glare at him, slightly offended that he would accuse me of something so cruel. "I would never play about something like this."

The smile fades from his face and he leans back in his seat. "Wow. Poor guy. I feel really sorry for him. So, how did he take your rejection?"

I take a deep breath in and exhale before saying, "I didn't reject him. I told him yes. Corey, I'm going to marry Morris."

He appears appalled. "What? This has got to be a joke. You're going to marry a man who's dying? Felicia, come on. I understand feeling bad for him, but you don't have to marry him."

"Yes, I do," I say, sorrowfully. "He's my best friend and he needs me right now. I don't expect you to understand all of this, but I had to tell you why I can't see you anymore."

The realization of what I'm saying to him must have hit him because he scowls at me in anger. "You're serious. You're really going to break up with me and marry him because he's dying. Felicia, this is crazy. Morris just doesn't like me. Don't let him ruin what we have. Have you even verified that any of this is true?"

"No, and I'm not going to," I say determinedly. "Morris isn't a liar and he would never ever use his illness as leverage with me. He just wants to experience marriage before he dies and I'm the only one who can make his last wish come true. I have to do this. I'm so sorry if my decision is hurting you in any way."

Corey gets up from his seat and comes around to my side of the table, sitting down next to me. "No. I'm not going to let you go. You can't just leave me like this."

I shake my head. "You have to let me go. If you care about me, you'll just let me do this."

"If you love me, you'll stay with me," he says, adamantly.

Hot tears burn my cheeks. "You know I love you, but I can't stay." I scoot over in the booth, forcing him to get up to let me out.

He towers over me, a dejected expression in his eyes. "Please don't."

I stand, and with tears falling from my eyes, I kiss him softly on the lips. He returns my kiss, sweetly and sadly. I pull away from him, look deeply into his eyes one final time, and say, "Goodbye, Corey."

"Felicia," he calls out to me, but I rush away from him, a table full of food, and one of our favorite restaurants. In that moment, I finally understand what Whitney Houston meant when she asked the question, *Where do broken hearts go?*

A Family Affair

Morris

Now that **we've agreed** upon where we will live and where the wedding will be, it's time to tell our families and friends, starting first with our parents.

Felicia and I decide to cook for our parents and have dinner over her house the following night. Neither of us being culinary experts, we keep it simple and prepare spaghetti and meatballs, with a Caesar salad, garlic bread, and peach cobbler for dessert. As we sit around the dinner table, I notice my parents and her parents exchanging glances at each other, most likely trying to figure out what's the big secret or surprise. We never cook for our parents, especially not a joint family dinner. I'd say it's obvious that we are warming them up for a bit of unexpected news.

Felicia isn't wearing her engagement ring. We agreed that she should keep it under wraps until we get the word out to those closest to us. We'd hate to have the town gossips tell our friends and family before we've had a chance to do so.

The majority of the meal is filled with small talk. My father asks Felicia about whether or not she still intends to move back to Boston. My mother questions her about if her and her boyfriend—"What's the fella's name?"—are considering marriage. Felicia's dad voices his disappointment with me resigning from his company. Felicia's mom concurs with his sentiments and probes about what I'll do now.

We both hem and haw through our responses, looking for the right moment—and the right way—to spill the beans. Finally, I take courage and put the whole room out of its misery—and anxiety.

"Felicia and I are getting married," I blurt out with very little tact.

"What? You're getting married?" my mother asks. "To who? I didn't know you were dating anyone."

I glance at Felicia who looks back at me, and we burst into a deep belly laugh. Our parents sit in silence as we give way to our giggles for about a minute, then wipe our eyes from the tears that have surfaced. It feels so good to laugh, to really laugh and mean it. There hasn't been much lately to laugh about, but this moment is definitely laugh worthy.

"Mom," I say, once I've regained my composure, "I'm marrying Felicia."

"Felicia?" her mother whom I refer to as Mrs. J. asks with budging eyes.

I nod humbly. "Yes, ma'am. I proposed to your daughter a couple of days ago, on her birthday."

"And I said yes," Felicia adds.

The room becomes quiet, pin-dropping quiet. I study the faces of the people around the table, trying to anticipate their reactions. Mrs. J. looks like a deer caught in headlights. I'm surprised because out of the Jefferson family, I thought she'd figure out my feelings for her daughter first. Maybe she had, she just didn't think her child would ever return them. Well, technically Felicia's feelings aren't the same as mine, but I'll take her love any way that I can get it.

Mr. J. has a small smile on his face. I know that he wants the best for his daughter, especially when it comes to marriage. I can't count how many times he's told me that he wishes Felicia would find a kind and trustworthy man like me. He's never cared for Corey Dillard; thinks the man is sneaky and not a good match for his baby girl. With my announcement, he seems to realize that his wish has come true. Corey is no more, and the good guy finally wins.

My dad appears startled. He knows that I've always been romantically interested in Felicia, but he never thought I'd man up and make her mine. So many times, he's given me the go-after-what-you-want pep talk. But my response was that I wanted her to be happy, even if that meant being with another man. He's slowed down on the lectures over the past year, probably feeling defeated. He's accepted that I would never make my move. I'm sure once he gets over the shock of the matter, he'll be proud of me.

My mother looks as if she just won a beauty pageant. Her hands are over her mouth, which is stuck in an "O" formation. Mom has been praying that I'll find a good wife. She wants grandchildren, and since I'm her only child, she's been nagging me about it since I turned eighteen. Of course, she is the one who breaks the silence.

"Oh my word! Are you serious? You two are getting married? That's wonderful!" she shrieks, stands up, and runs over to me then Felicia, hugging us and kissing us on our cheeks.

"I—I don't understand," Mrs. J. says "I mean, I'm happy for you two, but I thought that Felicia was dating Corey."

"Well, I'm glad she's no longer with Corey," Mr. J. says before either Felicia or I can respond. "Morris will make a much better husband for Felicia. Congratulations to you kids!"

"It's about time son," my dad says, finally speaking up. "I thought I'd take my last breath before you'd ever muster up the courage to ask Felicia on a date. I guess you skipped over asking for a date and just proposed!"

"Yes, he did," my mother said, merrily. "I want to know all of the details. How did he propose? Where's the ring? Morris, you didn't buy her a ring?"

I chuckle at my mother's excitement. "Yes, Mom, I bought her a ring. We wanted to wait until after we told everyone before she started wearing it around town."

"I'm still wondering what happened to Corey. I just saw you with him on your birthday," Mrs. J says, looking perplexed. "Does he know that you've decided to marry Morris?"

Felicia nods. "Yes, Mama. Corey knows. We've broken up."

Mrs. J. purses her lips. She doesn't appear disappointed, but at the same time, she's not thrilled about the news, not like everyone else. "Morris, please don't take offense to what I'm about to say. Felicia, it's not like you to be this impulsive. How could you break things off with one man and agree to marry another the same day?"

Felicia looks over at me and I give her a non-verbal cue that I don't want her to tell them the truth. I've chosen to keep my concerns about my failing health from my parents, and if she tells her mother the truth right here, right now, it will destroy my parents. I have to spoon feed my parents this harsh reality, one tough bite at a time.

"I know, Mama, but it was the right thing to do," Felicia says. "Morris is my best friend. I probably should have dated him a long time ago instead of some of these other guys that didn't treat me right. I've been honest with Corey about my decision and why it has to be this way. It's really for the best, trust me."

Mrs. J. lets out a reluctant sigh and says, "Okay. If this is what you want . . ."

"It's what I want," Felicia says, then reaches into her purse, which has been hanging on the back of her chair, and pulls out the diamond ring that I gave her. She places the ring back on her ring finger and waves her hand out in front of us so that everyone can see the sparkling rock.

"That's gorgeous," my mom says, ogling the precious stone.

"It's is. Well done, son," my dad compliments.

"I must agree," Mrs. J. says "It's a beautiful ring. Since we all seem to be coming in late to the party, have the two of you picked a date? If you want a spring or summer wedding, you'll have to start planning right away."

"November seventh," I say boldly, waiting for the next wave of shock to commence.

"Okay, that gives you two a little over a year to plan. I think that's a smart move," Mrs. J. says.

"No, Mama," Felicia says. "This November. Next month."

Gasps come from everyone in the room expect me and Felicia.

Mrs. J. tosses her dinner napkin onto the table. "That's ridiculous. No one can plan a wedding in a month, at least not an elegant one. Why are you rushing? Are—are you . . . pregnant?"

For the second time this evening, Felicia and I look at each other then burst into laughter. The situation is anything but funny, but the idea of her and I having a shotgun wedding is full of humor. I've never even gotten to second base with Felicia, and from what she's told me, she's still a virgin, so there's no way that she could be pregnant.

"No, Ma!" Felicia says through her chuckles. "We just don't want to waste any time."

I attempt to straighten my face and sound serious. "We're planning a small and simple ceremony with just close family and friends in the backyard of our new house."

"New house?" my father asks immediately.

I feel a bit guilty for keeping so many secrets from my parents. "I bought a house over on Bear Creek Road about a month ago. We'll be moving in after the wedding."

"You two have really planned this entire thing out, haven't you?" Mr. J. says. "I'm impressed. If there's anything that my wife and I can do to help you with the wedding or your new lives together, financially or otherwise, just let us know. We'd be happy to help. Right, dear?" He places his hand on his wife's shoulder.

She peers up at him and quickly submits. "Right . . . Of course."

"Well, I guess we need to move on to dessert. There's plenty to celebrate about tonight," my father says, concluding the matter.

Yes, there is a lot to celebrate, but between Felicia and I there are other issues that haven't been spoken that warrant no happy occasion at all.

Do You Take This Man?

Felicia

The month between my acceptance of Morris' proposal and our wedding day has flown by faster than I can say, "I do." November 7th has arrived, and I am clothed in my wedding dress, in the now furnished master bedroom of our new house, allowing my mother, sister, and close girlfriends to fuss over me. As Nikki, my hairstylist and good friend, pins up my curly hair, giving me a sophisticated up-do, I think about how much has occurred over the past month. Because time was of the essence, we emailed our save the dates a couple of days after the big reveal to our parents, then mailed out the invitations the following week. We asked our guests to either RSVP online via a wedding website we'd created, or to text message us their responses. We decided not to have bridesmaids or groomsmen, so shopping for dresses and tuxedos were limited to Morris and me.

I found a lovely yet simple ivory dress and matching shoes at a bridal boutique in Savannah, while Morris rented a tuxedo from a shop in Richmond Hill. We spent a weekend in Savannah, picking up wedding supplies and purchasing furniture for our new home. I can't believe the amount of money that was spent on everything, but Morris never batted an eye. I am not sure how much he has saved up, but it eases my anxiety to know that my parents are paying for the wedding. Morris didn't want to take their money, but I told him that it was the only way I'd feel comfortable with our deal, so he gave in.

Corey hasn't given up his quest to win me back. I want him to let me go. His carrying on the way he has only makes my decision harder to bear. I'm not backing out on Morris, so Corey's attempts to change my mind only causes me to feel guiltier about our breakup. Like three days ago when I *bumped* into him at the bank. He knows that on Wednesdays I go to the bank before going grocery shopping with my mom. Many of the local grocery stores offer one-day only specials on Wednesdays, so trolling the stores has become a routine for Mom and me. As I was exiting the bank, Corey was standing outside the door, waiting for me to walk past him.

Spotting him, I sucked in my breath and bravely approached him. "Corey," I said.

He grinned. He looked extremely handsome, more handsome than I remember. "Hello, Felicia. How are you?"

"I'm well. You?"

"I've been better," he said. "Much better when I was with you."

I huffed, not wanting to do the entire charade with him in front of the bank, in front of my mother who was watching from the passenger side of my car in the parking lot. "Corey, what do you want?"

"I want us. I miss you."

I rolled my eyes. "I'm getting married in three days."

"You don't have to. You can still walk away from this fake marriage."

"It's not fake."

"Do you love him?"

Good question, but I would never dignify it with an answer. "That's none of your business."

"Do you still love me?"

I peered up at him and his puppy dog eyes. Although he's one of the most adorable men I've ever met, I refused to be manipulated by his charm. "I have to go," I said, quickly looking away. "Take care of yourself."

I headed in the direction of my vehicle, wanting to drown him out. Unfortunately, my feet aren't fast enough, and I heard him say, "Felicia, even after you marry him, I'll still be here waiting for you to come back to where you belong."

My mom watched our entire exchange. When I hopped back into the car and started the engine, she asked, "Wasn't that Corey? What was that all about?"

I avoided making eye contact with her. "Yes, that's Corey. It was nothing, Mama. Resist the devil and he will flee."

My mom frowned at me, but I shrugged it off and drove out of the bank's parking lot.

I've tried not to think about that brief moment between Corey and I at the bank, and with all of the last minute preparations, it's been an easy thought to avoid. But now, looking at myself in the full length mirror, I question if I am doing the right thing. I hear Corey's words, "I miss you," over and over again in my mind. I miss him too, but admitting this openly, especially to him, would only borrow trouble. I am committed to Morris, committed to spending the rest of his life with him. Missing Corey doesn't matter, not anymore.

An hour passes, and I find myself in my new backyard, walking on top of a white cloth runner toward the gazebo and Morris. Music is playing softly in the background. I recognize it as "Here and Now" by Luther Vandross. I feel the small crowd staring at me, but my mind focuses on the words to the song. The chorus ends saying, "Your love is all I need." I can't agree with Luther. I'm actually marrying a man who I don't love or need. Well, maybe I do need him, but not in the marriage way. He needs me though, and he loves me.

By the time I work out my problems with my wedding song, I'm at the gazebo and mere inches away from Morris. My father hands me off to him, and it is in this moment I remember my father was with me as I walked down the aisle. I take Morris' hand as my mind plays with the words. *My father was with me. My Heavenly Father is with me always.* I equate the notion to mean that I am making the right choice.

I look up at Morris and he smiles at me. His smile is brilliant and I'm happy that I can make him happy. My fears ease and I pay attention to the words of his father, the Reverend Michael Bryson, as he officiates the ceremony.

"Dearly beloved, we are gathered here today in the presence of these witnesses, to join Morris Bryson and Felicia Jefferson in matrimony, which is commended to be honorable among all men . . ."

The ceremony moves quickly, and before I know it, we are at the question of intent.

Rev. Bryson smiles at me and asks, "Do you, Felicia Jefferson, take this man to be your husband, to live together in the covenant of marriage? Will you love him, comfort him, honor and keep him, in sickness and in health, and forsaking all others, be faithful to him as long as you both shall live?"

I glance at Morris and gulp before saying, "I do."

"And do you, Morris Bryson, take this woman to be your wife, to live together in the covenant of marriage? Will you love her, comfort her, honor and keep her, in sickness and in health, and forsaking all others, be faithful to her as long as you both shall live?"

Morris winks at me. "I do"

"Morris, please repeat after me," Rev. Bryson says, and Morris follows, gazing directly into my eyes.

"I, Morris Bryson, take thee, Felicia Jefferson, to be my wedded wife, to have and to hold from this day forward, for better for worse, for richer, for poorer, in sickness and in health, to love and to cherish, till death us do part, according to God's holy ordinance."

Rev. Bryson turns to me and says, "Felicia, please repeat after me."

I hear the vows he feeds me, and obediently repeat them.

"I, Felicia Jefferson, take thee, Morris Bryson, to be my wedded husband, to have and to hold from this day forward, for better for worse, for richer, for poorer, in sickness and in health, to love, cherish, and to obey, till death us do part, according to God's holy ordinance."

As we present each other with our wedding bands, we say the agreed upon words, "I give you this ring as a symbol of my love; and all my worldly goods I thee endow. With all that I am and all that I have, I honor you, in the name of the Father, and of the Son, and of the Holy Spirit."

A few other ceremonial activities occur, including the lighting of the unity candle, a song, and a prayer. Then Rev. Bryson says the words we've been anticipating since I first agreed to marry Morris. "By the power vested in me by the State of Georgia, I now pronounce you husband and wife. You may now kiss the bride."

Morris grins at me and I'm pretty sure what he's thinking. The last time we kissed, we were teenagers, coming home from the senior prom. That was almost twenty years ago. Kissing him again will be awkward, especially since no one besides us knows that our marriage isn't the fairytale everyone else believes it is. Morris takes a step closer to me, leans in, and kisses me softly and innocently. When he backs away, I bite my bottom lip, feeling somewhat embarrassed by our public display of affection.

Rev. Bryson smiles brightly and says, "It is my pleasure to present to you for the first time, Mr. and Mrs. Morris Bryson."

Hand-in-hand with Morris, we turn to face the crowd who is now cheering and applauding. I didn't know if I could really do this, but somehow I have. I've married my next door neighbor. I've married my best friend. Maybe married life, even without being in love, won't be so bad after all.

For Better or for Worse

Morris

Maybe I'm too much of a dreamer. I imagined that once we got married, our relationship would smooth out. Felicia would realize that she really did love me, and would allow herself to enjoy the beautiful home and lifestyle that I'd given her. For some reason, that isn't the direction our relationship is going.

I am scared to say the words, but I think she resents me. Maybe she's having second thoughts about giving up Corey Dillard and marrying me. She hasn't said so, but her actions demonstrate that emotionally, she is unavailable to me.

We spent our first couple of nights as husband and wife at home before heading to our week long honeymoon in New Smyrna Beach, Florida, a coastal community about fifteen minutes south of Daytona. Using her parents' time share, we stayed in a beachfront condo, giving us the chance to see the sunrise every morning beyond the endless stretch of Atlantic Ocean. Although our trip was relaxing for me, Felicia was tense the entire time. We slept in the same bed, but I didn't dare to touch her. She was cold and distant. Despite the fact that she is my wife and according to the Bible her body is mine and mine is hers, I won't force her to be sexually intimate with me. I don't want her to heartlessly give her virginity away to me. If we ever engage in sex, I want it to be because she wants to be with me, not just because she married me.

By the time we return back to Georgia, I am frustrated. Felicia and I were closer when we were just friends. I start to wonder if marriage will kill what remains of our lifelong friendship. I'm agitated because she won't open up to me, and my emotions are beginning to show in the way I talk to her. I've always been able to speak gently and kindly to her, but the last few days, I've found myself being unusually harsh.

"Do you want to return to work?" I ask her as she lies in the far end of our bed, as far as she can away from me. We've just retired for the night, so even though the lights are off, I know she's not asleep yet.

"No. You asked me not to work, so I won't," she says defiantly.

I'm tired of playing this passive-aggressive game with her. I can't—no, I won't have a marriage like this. I turn my body toward hers. "Felicia, what's wrong? Just tell me so that we can work through it."

"Nothing's wrong."

I sigh deeply. "You're lying. I'm your best friend. I know you're upset or sad or resentful, but you're not fine. I'm sorry if being married to me has ruined your life."

"You haven't ruined my life," she says quietly.

"Then why are you acting like this?" I ask, my voice a bit pained. "We spend an entire week in Florida on the beach and you sulk the entire time. What do you want from me?"

I hear her suck her teeth. "Nothing."

I can't help but feel offended. "So that's it, huh? There's nothing I have that you want or even need. Tell the truth."

"Go to bed, Morris," she says.

I won't back down. "Just tell me the truth," I insist.

"I don't want to have this conversation right now."

"Just tell me the truth!" I growl.

"No," she says tersely. "There's nothing that you have that I want or need. Are you happy?"

I lie flat on my back. How did we get here so quickly? Less than two weeks ago, we were saying our vows, agreeing to honor and cherish each other. Now we couldn't even have a conversation without hurting each other's feelings. "I thought I would be," I say, staring up into the dark. "I thought marrying you would make me the happiest man in the world. But if this marriage is going to make you miserable, which will then make me miserable, we can get it annulled."

I hear her shift in the bed. "What?"

I don't want to offer her a way out of our marriage, but I also don't want to spend the little life I have left arguing with the woman I love. I'd rather let her go. "We haven't consummated the marriage yet, so I'm sure that it would be easy to annul it."

She is quiet for about a minute, then says, "I didn't say that I no longer wanted to be married to you."

I close my eyes. "Well, when you figure out what it is that you want, you let me know and I'll do whatever you want."

I fall asleep wondering if she leaves me will she run back to Corey Dillard.

Forsaking All Others

Felicia

My attitude is crappy and I know it. I don't mean to be difficult, especially toward Morris, but for some reason, I can't help it. I felt optimistic at our wedding like there was hope for us, hope for our future together. I danced and laughed and ate cake at the reception like a blushing bride should. I thought I would lose my virginity that night, and I was scared to death about it, but Morris was a gentleman and didn't push up on me in that way. Instead, he held me through the night as if we had pretended to get married and were now back to just being buddies.

That night, I dreamed of Corey. Instead of Morris, Corey and I were getting married. And the messed up part was that I was truly happy. As I walked down the aisle and Luther Vandross sang that Corey's love was all I needed, I agreed and I believed him. During the vows, I gazed at him in awe and meant every word that I recited. Till death us do part.

I awoke the next day in a funk. I pulled Morris' arms off me and immediately erected an invisible wall between us. It wasn't Morris' fault that I wasn't in love with him, but I couldn't stop ruminating that I had somehow chosen obligation over true love, sympathy over my heart's desire.

It's now the day after Morris extended to me the opportunity to annul our marriage. I didn't sleep a wink last night. I kept thinking about whether or not I should take him up on his offer. I could walk away from our marriage with my virginity still intact and marry Corey, the man I really want to be with. Like Lauryn Hill says in the song "Ex-Factor," *It could all be so simple.*

As easy as it sounds, I'm not convinced that leaving Morris is the best route. I want to make an informed decision about my marriage, but the only way to get the information that I need to choose wisely is to see Corey again and give him a chance to tell me how he feels about me. There's no use in delaying the inevitable, so I go to Corey's practice to see him. It's around lunchtime and his receptionist tells me that he's gone up to the sandwich shop down the road to grab a bite to eat. I thank her for the info and drive over to the plaza with the sandwich shop in question. I see his vehicle parked outside the place and know that he's inside. My heart begins to race as I consider what I'm going to say to him. I grab my purse, but before I step out of the car, I see him exit the shop with an attractive, young woman. They are smiling at each other. I know that smile; it's the smile he used to give me. I remain inside my car and watch their interaction. They talk back and forth for a few minutes, both of them seeming engrossed in each other. At one point, he glances around the parking lot, but to my chagrin, he doesn't even notice my car or the fact that I'm sitting inside it. After several minutes, they part ways, but before they do, they embrace and kiss. My heart plummets. Not even two whole months have passed since we broke up and he already has another lady in his life. Less than three weeks ago, at the bank, he promised he would wait for me. Yet, he didn't wait. He's moved on and I'm left feeling crushed.

I can't blame him; it's my fault. I broke up with him. I married another man. I did this to us.

I take a drive through the country to clear my head. I let myself cry, hard. My life feels like it's in shambles and I'm not sure how to put it back together again.

"God, what do I do?" I ask my Maker.

In the midst of my tears, I see a sign on a building that cuts to my core.

HOME IS WHERE THE HEART IS.

I know the message is meant for me. It's the divine answer I need at this very moment. I don't know what will happen next, but I have enough faith to believe that all things are working together for my good. Resolved, I wipe my eyes, turn the vehicle around, and head back home.

To Have and to Hold

Morris

I don't know what happened, but Felicia comes
home and immediately hugs me. This is the same
woman who hasn't allowed me to touch her since
the day after our wedding, and now, she's hugging
me. If I'd known that all I'd have to do to regain her
affection was offer her an annulment, I would have
said the words on day one of our honeymoon.

"I'm so sorry, Morris," she says, still embracing
me. "I don't want an annulment. I want to stay with
you until the end."

I lift her face up so that I can see her eyes; they
are red and swollen. She's been crying. My heart
breaks at the thought that possibly something I've
said or done is causing her so much grief.

"Are you okay?" I ask. "What happened?"

She shakes her head. "It just took me a little
time to realize where home is."

Her statement causes my heart to leap. Could it be that she's ready to give herself completely to this marriage? "Are you sure?"

"Yes," she says. "Please forgive me for treating you so badly. I don't understand why all of this is happening to us, why we're in such a crazy situation, but I know that God is with us and He never puts more on us than we can bear."

Her words touch my soul and I pull her in for a tighter embrace. I thank God for every victory—big and small—and today, we've won our first major battle as husband and wife.

Felicia

Morris and I continue to grow closer and fonder of each other over the following week. By Thanksgiving, I am beginning to feel like a real wife. We still haven't consummated the marriage, but I've enjoyed getting to know him in a different way, as a life partner and not just a friend. I'm surprised that he hasn't even mentioned the fact that we aren't having sex, but then again, Morris is a respectable man who wouldn't want me to feel pressured to be intimate. I have to admit, over the past day or so, I've begun to wonder what it would be like to give myself to him. He's an attractive man and I've never felt so loved by any other man in my life, with the exception of my father. I've started to pray about the matter, asking God if I should take our relationship to this next level and when. It might sound silly that I would ask God these questions, but Morris and I didn't marry for typical reasons and I just don't want to waste thirty-five years of purity because of lust or curiosity. I want my heart, mind, body, and soul all on one accord.

Morris and I host Thanksgiving Day dinner at our home. Our parents, along with my sister, her husband and children join us for the occasion. The meal is wonderful, with all of the women pitching in to make savory soul food that pays homage to our ancestors. At one point in the afternoon, Stacy and I end up in the kitchen alone, and I'm grateful. It gives me a chance to open up to her with my thoughts about going all of the way with Morris. I slide close to her near the sink where she's washing dishes. Everyone is stuffed from dinner, and the men are watching football while our mothers separate and box up the leftovers so that each family can take food home.

"Stacy," I say as I start to assist her by drying the dishes she has washed, "I need your advice."

"What's up, sis?" she asks without looking up from the sudsy water.

I feel a bit foolish, but I'm itching to talk to her. She's a married woman, she should know about these things. "How do you know when it's the right time to . . . you know . . . have sex with your husband?"

Her head jerks up at me and she eyes me like I've just lost my mind. "What kind of question is that? You act as if there's a wrong time."

I shrug. "Isn't there?"

"Not really," she says with a girlish giggle. "The marriage bed is undefiled. You have the right to have sex with your husband whenever you two want. Why are you asking this? Does Morris want it too much or something?"

"I wouldn't say that. I'm embarrassed to admit it, but I need to talk to someone so bad about this or I'm going to burst. Morris and I haven't had sex yet." I bite my bottom lip.

She winces. "You're joking, right?"

"Unfortunately, I'm not."

She drops the plate she is washing into the soapy water and turns toward me. "Why not? You two have been married almost a month now. I'm sure you've had plenty of opportunities to make the magic happen. Is something wrong with his . . . ?"

"Stacy!" I scold her then look around to make sure no one has entered the kitchen. "No, nothing is wrong; at least I don't think so."

She places a wet hand on her hip. "Well then, why are you two playing around? I'm tempted to go in that living room and order you two to go to your bedroom and stay there until the deed is done. You've got all of these single folks running around here having premarital sex and babies and whatnot, and you married people act like you're scared of the word sex, at least when it comes to the person you're married to. Unless there's some medical issue preventing the two of you from rolling in the sack, I suggest you get with the program and enjoy *all* of the benefits of marriage."

I find myself still mulling over her words as Morris and I climb into bed. Am I missing out on the benefits of marriage by keeping my body from my husband? Although our marriage is a bit unorthodox, we are technically married in both the eyes of the law and the eyes of God. What am I waiting for?

I know Morris will never initiate sex with me until he knows that I'm interested in being with him in this manner. I'll have to make the first move, but I feel so unexperienced and unprepared. Should we use protection like condoms or birth control pills? Do married people even care about prophylactics? This was a question I forgot to ask Stacy, but it's now well after 10:00 p.m. and if I got out of the bed and called her with this concern, Morris would wonder what I am up to and Stacy would yell at me for interrupting her sleep. I decide to pass on more advice from Stacy and take matters into my own hands.

I turn on my night stand's lamp and move closer to Morris, kissing him quickly on his lips. For a second, I want to laugh because I'm acting like a child, not a 35-year-old married woman.

Morris keeps his eyes closed, but smiles at my gesture.

"Night, Felicia," he says groggily.

I know it's been a long day for the both of us and that he's probably ready to pass out, but I won't be able to get any sleep until we consummate this marriage. It has to happen tonight.

"Morris," I say.

"Um hmm," he mumbles.

"I . . . I think we should go there."

"Go where?"

"You know . . . there."

"Where's there?" he asks.

I huff in frustration. I don't want to sound crass, but I'll have to paint a clearer picture. "There. Sex. I think we should have sex."

His eyes shoot open. "Did you just say what I think you said 'cause I think you said something that I'm not sure you said? Did I drift off and just dream that?"

I laugh. "No, Morris. You're not dreaming. I said what you think I said. I think we should have sex or at least try to. I mean, we're married, right?"

He nods and appears . . . eager. "Yeah, we're married. Are—are you sure you want to . . . with me?"

I smile at him and say, "I couldn't think of someone more deserving."

We make love for the first time. Some may call it sex, but I say it's love because I know he loves me and I do it because I love him.

I've finally given him the best of me, all of me. There's no turning back now.

To Love, Comfort, and Obey

Felicia

My relationship with Morris grows in leaps and bounds. We continue to be intimate and it seems that our physical connection helps evolve our well-developed friendship into something greater—romantic love. Over time, I begin to tell him that I love him and I no longer mean it platonically. I've somehow fallen in love with my husband, Morris Bryson, and the news that I am carrying his child only three months after our wedding, strengthens my desire for him even more.

The months pass and our affection, as well as my belly, grow and grow until the day comes that I feel I am going to burst—and I do. November 10th, one year after our vows, I give birth to twins, a boy and a girl. He names them Morris Landon Bryson II and Faith Monique Bryson.

"Morris, aren't twins supposed to have similar names? Morris and Faith aren't even close to similar," I complain.

Morris is sitting in a chair next to my bedside, holding Faith, while Morris II is cradled in my arms.

"Twins don't have to have similar names. I don't know who made up that rule. And besides, Faith's middle name is Monique. That's close to Morris."

"That's doesn't make sense. Most people won't even know what her middle name is. Why Faith?"

"Because the 'F' is for Felicia, and these children are a product of our faith in God."

I can't argue with that rationale. Who would have ever guessed that Morris and I would be happily married with two kids? All we needed was a dog and a white picket fence and we would be the American dream. Morris is right. Faith is the perfect name for our newborn daughter.

Morris

I can't believe I'm a father. I find myself repeatedly giving thanks to God for the miracle of not one baby, but two. Me, a man who was told fourteen months ago that I should make the most of my life because I wouldn't live much longer, not only has a nice home, but a beautiful wife that finally loves me the way I love her, and precious babies that will carry on my legacy. I'm in awe by God's favor, grace, and mercy.

Since the birth of my children, I constantly catch myself staring at my family. I'm blessed, but the still quiet voice within tells me that my time is short. When the doctor first urged me to live my life to the fullest, there were experiences I wanted to have like marriage, but if God would have taken my life then, I would have gone without a complaint. Now, I have so much to live for that I hate the idea of leaving it all behind. So many questions fill my mind. *Who will raise my children? Will another man make love to my wife? What man will fill my shoes? Will it be Corey Dillard or someone else? How do I know that when I'm gone my family will be okay?*

Initially I believed that as long as I tucked away some money and made sure Felicia had a house and a bank account, my death would not be a traumatic loss. Life would go on without me and although some tears might be shed on my behalf, the world would keep on turning as if I never existed. But now I realize how delusional I really was. I do exist and my babies are proof of my time here on earth. When I die, lives will be affected, and no amount of money or security can replace my presence.

I've been feeling weaker lately. I haven't mentioned it to Felicia, but she's always watching me and I have a feeling that she knows. I've been praying to God like Hezekiah, asking God to add fifteen years to my life. I have prayed Isaiah 38:3 faithfully since the birth of my children.

Remember now, O LORD, I beseech thee, how I have walked before thee in truth and with a perfect

*heart, and have done that which is good in thy
sight.*

I have waited patiently for a sign that God has
heard me and will change my outcome. I long to
hear the words, *"I have heard thy prayer, I have
seen thy tears: behold, I will add unto thy days
fifteen years."*

But day after day, the voice of God seems silent.

And then, on Christmas Eve, I hear His voice
and He is clear.

**"To every thing there is a season, and a time to
every purpose under the heaven: a time to be born,
and a time to die."**

In Sickness and in Health

Morris

Our parents come to our house on Christmas Day. We spent last Christmas at Felicia's parents' house, but with the babies, it was mutually decided that the gathering would take place at our abode. I'd been pacing the floor since 3:00 a.m., begging God for a different answer and trying to figure out what to do next.

Why?

Why me?

Why now?

I'd never questioned God about my illness in the past. Even growing up with so much pain and all of the hospital stays, I never complained to God about this cross I have to bear. But now, I can't help but feel resentful, like I got the bad end of the stick. I know that God has a perfect plan, but why does it feel like the ones who love Him are often the ones that suffer the most.

I'm not strong about this and I won't pretend to be. I realize that I have to come clean with my parents, and I guess Christmas is as good of a time to tell them as any. The true meaning of Christmas is Jesus' birth and the hope of everlasting life. It is with this promise that I try to find the silver lining in my dilemma.

After an early dinner and exchanging of gifts, I take Felicia's hand and address our parents.

"Mom, Dad, Mr. and Mrs. J. I need to tell you some difficult news," I begin. "I love and appreciate this woman for marrying me, and I am eternally grateful that she has learned to love me with her whole heart and honor me by having my children."

"Oh, that's sweet," my mom says, interrupting my speech.

"There's more. I haven't been completely honest with you all," I say. Felicia looks up at me and nods, letting me know that she understands what I'm about to do.

"Felicia didn't marry me because she was head over heels in love with me. And she didn't breakup with Corey Dillard because he wasn't right for her. She married me because I asked her to do me a huge favor. About a year and a half ago, my doctor let me know that the sickle cell anemia has caused a lot of damage to my organs and that I probably won't live much longer. He urged me to make the most out of whatever time I had left."

"What?" my mother shrieks.

I can see the pain and shock on all of their faces, but I continue to tell my story. It's the only way I'll get it all out without breaking down. "I wanted to experience marriage, having a home of my own, possibly even a family, so I told Felicia about my situation and asked her to marry me."

"Oh, Lord! Why didn't you tell us?" Mrs. J. cries out.

"Felicia is such a good friend that she broke up with Corey and sacrificed herself to make my dreams come true. Thank God, she eventually started to actually enjoy being married to me," I say. I smile at her, yet tears are watering my eyes.

"I'm telling you all this because I don't think I have much time left. This will probably be my last Christmas with you all and I . . ." I choke up. "I need you all to know how much I love you and . . . how much I'll need you to be there for my wife and children once I'm gone."

If I never knew how much I mean to others, this moment shows me how much I am loved. The room explodes with sobbing, hugs, questions, and mourning. I don't want to ruin their holiday, so I say, "I don't want my last Christmas to be a sad one. I know I can't take back what I just told you all, but if we can, let's focus our minds on the greatness of a God who has made so many sacrifices to give us life. He is still in control and He is still amazing. My life will go on even after death because of Him."

Felicia embraces me and says, "He is with us. He will never leave us. He will never forsake us."

Till Death Us Do Part

Morris

In January, my health takes a turn for the worse. The day I woke up in agony from a sickle cell crisis, I had a feeling that I was heading in a downhill direction and would never travel to higher heights in this life again. A trip to the emergency room, followed by a lengthy hospital stay and a battery of tests confirm my suspicions—I am diagnosed with multiple organ failure. The damage to my organs is irreparable, and it is only a matter of time before my system completely shuts down.

I am placed in hospice care, and Felicia and I agree that I should come home for my final days. I want to be around my children and bringing them up to a hospital or nursing home isn't healthy for them. I feel so guilty for the fact that I'll be leaving them without a father, even guiltier about Faith whose blood tests shows significant levels of abnormal hemoglobin, suggesting a sickle cell anemia diagnosis. Previously unbeknownst to me, Felicia's father carries the sickle cell trait and passed it down to her. With me having the disease and her having the trait, any children of ours would have a 50 percent chance of inheriting the disease. Morris II's tests are normal, but it's likely that he may have inherited the sickle cell trait. Because of my disease, we were counseled about the risks associated with the pregnancy once Felicia started prenatal care. But learning from my experience, we agreed that our children were worth taking a risk on, and that we would leave the verdict on their health in God's hands. I was glad my mother didn't count me out before I was born, and I felt my children deserved the same chance. I am now thankful that I named my daughter Faith, because if her life is anything like mine, it's going to take a whole lot of trusting in the Lord to make it through the rough days.

Felicia pines over me day and night. I love her commitment to me, but I hate that her life revolves around tending to me. Sometimes, I want to order her to leave the house with the kids and stay away all day, but I would miss them too much. Being in this position forces me to lay aside my pride and accept the goodness of others. It's crazy how we often must be at the end of our ropes before we'll let others serve us.

Tonight, we are lounging in the family room in front of the fireplace. The children have fallen asleep, and Felicia and I are sipping hot chocolate, listening to jazz, and watching the burning embers get sucked up the chimney.

"Do you regret it?" I ask her.

She looks up at me innocently. "Regret what?"

"This. Us. Me."

"Uh, let me think," she says then giggles. "Of course not. It's the best decision I could have made. I didn't realize it at the time, but it was really all for my good."

"And for His glory," I say, reminding her.

"And for His glory," she repeats. "Do you regret it?"

I pull her closer into my arms. "Not one bit. This past year and a half has been the best time of my life. You know how people say that you save the best for last? Well, I feel like the best has been saved for last in my life. Thirty-seven years of life and the best moments happened at the end."

She frowns. "You know I hate when you refer to the end."

I plant a kiss on her cheek. "I know, but there's no use in denying it. I'd rather enjoy every second I have left because each is a blessing."

She sits up and looks at me in awe. "How can you be so strong about all of this? Even that first night that you told me, the night that you proposed, I kept thinking how strong you were. If it were me, I'd be laid out on this floor right now, cutting a fool."

I laugh as I imagine her rolling around the floor, kicking and screaming.

"Well, for one, it is you going through this and you're handling it very well. You and I are one, so you carry my struggle just as much as I do," I say.

She sighs. "I never thought about it like that."

"Felicia, you are full of strength. It's one of the reasons I fell in love with you. Being strong isn't about not crying or appearing unfathomed; it's about being willing to stick in the battle when everyone else has already given in. Not only did you rise to the occasion and marry your best friend who was dying and needed your love and support badly, but you take care of me and our children without complaining. So many women would hire other folks to do what you do. Pass the kids off to a nanny or grandma, get a few hospice workers in here to watch me around the clock, or even stick me in a nursing home even though I asked to die in my own house. You're faithful. That's strength to me."

She lies in my arms. "Thank you for saying that. I'll need to remember that when . . . when I no longer have you here by my side."

I rub her back. "Like you always say, God is with you even if I'm not. That's the other thing that gives me strength, knowing that there's more. I know some people don't believe in the afterlife, but knowing that there is a better place waiting for me makes it easier for me to let go of what I have here. I wish I could be here with you all forever, but since I can't, at least I know where I'm headed will be just as amazing as loving you."

Felicia

Despite the doctor's predictions, Morris lives to see his 38th birthday in March. I can tell he is getting weaker by the day, but he's a tough cookie and he won't go out without a fight. I plan a celebration for him, and family and friends alike come to the house to wish him a happy birthday. I wish I could do more, but by this point he is mostly confined to the bed we've set up in the family room for him. Since the bed arrived, I've abandoned our bedroom as well, sleeping next to him in the less luxurious hospital style bed. Yet I couldn't care less about the style of bed, I'm just grateful to spend more nights close to him.

The birthday party is bittersweet. I enjoy seeing so many people show love and respect for Morris, but when he blows out the candle on his cake—I only put one candle on the cake so he won't have to exert too much energy—I'm certain his wish is for me and the kids, and not himself. By the time everyone leaves our home, he is exhausted. I tuck both him and the babies into their beds before going outside into the backyard for a few minutes to get some fresh air. I stroll over to the gazebo, remembering our wedding day and the vows that we made. Till death us do part. I always thought that when my husband and I parted we would be old and gray, not shy of our forties.

It's a cool night, and I pull my sweater jacket closed to keep me warm. I know that I can't stay outside for too long. *What if one of the babies wake up crying? What if Morris stirs and needs me, but I'm not there?* For the past few months I've been everything to everybody, and I can't deny that I'm depleted. Our families come by often to help out and give me a break, but it's difficult for me to stay away from Morris for too long. I'm afraid that I'll sleep too long or travel too far and miss his last breath. I have to be with him to the very end. I need to hear him say goodbye, and I need to say it too.

The thought of missing any time with him, even as he sleeps, leads me back into the house. I find him quietly snoring, and I sigh in relief. He's still here. He's still with me.

April, May, and June fly by and Morris stays with me. He gets to kiss me and give me a rose on Mother's Day. I get to kiss him and give him cards 'from the twins' on Father's Day. I thank God for each dawn that I feel his heart beating and each dusk that I can wrap my arms around his thinning torso. I never want us to end.

On July 7th, exactly one year and eight months after our "I dos," I feel him slipping away from me. His breath is much more shallow than usual, and I quickly call the doctor and our families. I know in my heart that the end has come.

While we are still alone and waiting for others to arrive, he reaches out and touches my face. I kiss his hand and then kiss his lips, wanting so much to reach into the spiritual realm and pull him away from the forces that are enticing him from this world.

"I love you," I cry. "I'm so in love with you. You were always the one for me, even when I was too blind to see it. You will always live in my heart. I won't let you die there."

He tries to smile but his face barely moves upward. "You . . . are the most . . . beautiful . . . woman in the world. I'm . . . blessed to . . . have loved you. I . . . will watch over you . . . and save you . . . a place in heaven. Kiss my . . . children for me . . . and let them know . . . I love them. I love you . . . with my whole heart."

"I love you too, Morris. Please know that I love you so much," I say then rest my head on his chest. "Goodbye, Morris."

He touches my back. "Goodbye, Felicia," he says.

The room is quiet. I can hear his heart beat slowing. I don't dare to speak because I can't afford to miss this moment. I want his last words to me to be as they are. So I hold him closely as the breath leaves his body and his soul passes from this life into the next.

Tears fall from my eyes down to the remaining shell of my husband. Minutes pass and I stay gripping him, even when his parents and my parents rush into the house with the medical team. They have to pull me from him; I refuse to let go on my own. This is the man who has been there for me my entire life. How am I supposed to live without him?

Everything I Need

Felicia

I thought I could handle this twisted reality, but I can't. Nothing or no one can console me. I feel as if someone has reached into my chest and snatched out my heart. I promised myself that when God took Morris away that I'd be grateful and understanding, but it's a promise that I cannot keep. I am mad at God; I am furious. Why did I have to fall so deep in love, especially now? Why couldn't we have loved each other earlier in life so I would have had more time? What was the point of the delay if it was only going to end tragically?

I am so distraught that I can't hold my babies. My mother and sister take charge over the twins while I mourn the death of their father. I'm 36-years-old and a widow. I'm a single mother. This is not how my life was supposed to turn out.

The funeral is held less than a week later and I am a complete basket case. Ushers have to practically carry me into my father-in-law's church and seat me in the front pew. The casket is open and it takes everything in me not to run over to it and wrap my arms around his lifeless body. I am near catatonic until a soloist gets up and sings "Precious Lord, Take My Hand." My first thought is, *Who decided that this song would be the official funeral song for all black people?* But then the songstress gets to the part where she belts out, "Precious Lord, take my hand, lead me home," and I breakdown into uncontrollable sobs. I cry for my son and daughter who will never get to know their father. I cry for his parents who have outlived their only child. I cry for myself, who has lost my best friend. And I cry for Morris, who honored his mother and father and therefore should have lived a very long life.

I think my pain cannot overtake me any further, but when they close the lid on the casket, the smidge of strength left in me departs and with a heartbroken wail, I pass out.

By our anniversary, I've come to terms with this new chapter in my life. The past four months have been trying, but I've survived by the grace of God. I never thought I was the type to fall out at a funeral, but I surprised myself with the dramatic show I put on. Five minutes and a bit of fresh air brought me to and I was able to get through the cemetery section of the service without causing another scene— barely.

Following the funeral, I set my anger against God. How could One so loving hurt my family so deeply? If God is all-powerful, why didn't He spare Morris' life? Why do bad things happen to good people? I was full of unanswered questions, and the only One who could heal my broken heart was the One I'd blamed my sorrows on.

I wouldn't go to church, wouldn't read my Bible, and hated anyone and anything that tried to comfort me with words about God's greatness. He wasn't so great in my book—or at least, didn't act like it.

Eventually, I regained control over my emotions and my family trusted me enough to let me resume custody of my children. I was still salty with the Lord, but I wasn't as vocal with my complaints. I refused to pray, even over a meal. What was the point? God didn't answer prayers anyway.

But then, something happened, something wonderful. While going through Morris' closet, I found a box with my name on it. I opened it up and it was filled with letters that he wrote to me over the years, letters that I had never seen. I tried to put them in order by date; they went as far back as our pre-teen years. He wrote them in a journaling like fashion, but instead of addressing them as "Dear Journal" or "Dear God," they started with "Dear Felicia." He wrote about his day and confessed the times the he'd watched me from his bedroom window. He wrote to me his hopes and dreams;

many of them are about me and our lives together. I'm amazed by his love for me over the years, even when I was far off, living in Boston.

It took me a week to read through all of the letters. I laughed, sighed, and cried at the story of a man with a singular purpose—to love me.

His final letter was dated on New Year's Day. I hold it as if it is one of our babies, afraid to mishandle it in any way. It reads:

Dear Felicia,

If you are reading this letter, I am no longer with you and our children. I hope that you find this box of letters soon after I pass. I've been saving them for you, to one day share with you all of the things I never could. Everyone has a reason for being. God gives each one of us a mission in life, some way to positively influence the world and the people in it. He wants us all to spread His light, to reveal to others a glimpse of who He is and how He loves. My mission was to love you.

It might sound crazy, but love is a life changer. Loving you changed my life, and eventually changed yours too. There is so much left for you to accomplish in this world, but you have to be full of love to do it. I've spent the majority of my life pouring love into you so that one day, you'd be overflowing enough to shine your light of love into the lives of others. Your story will change lives as mine has changed yours.

I pray that you don't fall victim to self-pity and depression. Yes, our romance had an expiration date, but what we've built doesn't have to die just because my physical body did. Open your heart to all that still awaits you and you'll see the beauty beneath the pain.

I write this letter on New Year's Day because I'm certain I won't live to see another one. But you will. You will live to see so many more years and sunrises and sunsets. Appreciate them all and know that wherever I am, I take you and our children with me. Remember, God is with you. Love never fails.

Your husband and friend,
Morris

That day and that letter brought me back from the dead. When Morris died, I died with him. We were one flesh, so it made sense that I lost myself in him. But my life didn't start with him and it won't end with him. There's only One who has that position in my life, and the moment I realized this truth, I ran back to the lover of my soul.

Today, on our two year wedding anniversary, I visit Morris' gravesite and put fresh flowers out for him. I've brought the twins who are days away from their first birthday. From the looks of it, Morris II will be a spitting image of his daddy. The thought alone is awesome and scary at the same time.

Morris was true to his word and has left quite a bit of money for me and the kids. He said I could work again after he was gone, but I decide to stay at home with my children and raise them to be amazing, just like their father.

I leave the cemetery and get a craving for spaghetti. I laugh as I think about the spaghetti dinner Morris and I served our parents before telling them about our engagement. Going with the desire, I head over to the grocery store to pick up ingredients to make a big pot of spaghetti. I think I'll call my parents and in-laws and invite them over for dinner.

I am walking down the aisle of the grocery store with an extra-large buggy that somehow fits both babies and the few grocery items I've picked up, when I run into who else but Corey Dillard.

"Felicia?" he asks. His eyes are wide as if he's seeing a ghost.

"Long time no see, Corey," I say. It's true. The last time I saw him was that day in the plaza by the sandwich shop. What was that, almost two years ago?

"Yeah. It's great to see you. You look good," he says. "I heard about Morris. I'm truly sorry for your loss."

"Thank you," I say. "I appreciate your kind words. He's missed dearly."

He glances down at the two sleepy children in my cart. "Are these your kids?"

I nod. "Yes, they are. Morris the second and Faith."

"Wow, they're beautiful children."

I smile as any proud parent would. "Thanks. How have you been?"

"Good, everything's good," he says confidently. "The practice is growing. Business is good. What more can I say?"

"That's wonderful. You deserve it."

He steps closer, but not too close, and says in a low voice, "You know, I never got over you. I've tried to date other women, but they are just not you. I'm not sure if it's too soon or if you're still even interested, but I'd love to take you out sometime."

Morris would turn over in his grave if he knew that Corey Dillard was hitting on me in the grocery store. I laugh at the thought of Morris' reaction, not at Corey. "That's sweet, but yeah, it's too soon. One day I might be ready to open my heart again to romance, but for now, I think I'm just going to appreciate the love I already have."

The funny thing is I really mean these words. For the first time in my life I realize, I have everything I need.

Wife without a Ring

Shawna Claxton couldn't care less about capturing the coveted promotion at her job or having a fulfilling career. There is only one position she wants and has waited her entire life to get—to be a housewife. Though her friends think she is old fashioned, her current beau, NFL kicker Andy Tate, loves the idea. But when Andy finally proposes—in an unromantic way and without a ring—Shawna finds herself engaged in a very public battle between getting the man and getting the bling.

Wife Insurance

Wealthy resort owner, Cole Haven, is supposed to get married on Christmas to Violet, the woman he's been engaged to for the past five years. Yet, the same problem that has kept him from committing to the ceremony once again gives him an impossible case of cold feet—his distrust for women due to the actions of his ex-wife, Sophia. When Sophia hits him with an unreasonable ultimatum a month before his holiday wedding, and Violet is unwilling to compromise this Christmas, Cole will have to choose between taking a leap of faith or using the past as an indicator for what the future holds. If only he had a bit of wife insurance to guarantee him that marriage to Violet won't be the second biggest mistake of his life...

Wife for a Day

Isabella James and Myles Wright believe they have what it takes to succeed as a married couple. They have been dating for a year and can't wait to say their vows. However, their wedding plans are put on hold by Reverend Holley, a world renowned preacher who mandates that in order to marry them, the couple has to enroll in and pass Hard Knocks Marriage Boot Camp's Fully Engaged Weekend. Feeling sentimentally attached to Rev. Holley, the couple agrees to his requirements, unaware that the final and most difficult test during the weekend is a mock day of married life. With unexpected, real-life obstacles steadily being dropped on them, and feelings of frustration growing unbearable as the hours pass, will Isabella and Myles survive 24 hours of matrimony to prove their commitment, or will the marriage boot camp turn their forever into never?

About the Author

 **A'ndrea J. Wilson** is the author of over twenty books, including the award-winning Wife 101 series. A'ndrea dates her writing career back to high school where she majored in creative writing at Rochester, New York's School of the Arts. After graduation, she pursued careers in psychology and education, earning a Master's degree in Marriage and Family Counseling and a Ph.D. in Educational Leadership. An avid reader, she could never shake her passion for books, which eventually led to her penning her first manuscript. Her continuously growing body of faith-based work primarily focuses on integrating her clinical background and interest in relationship development with fiction; however, she also writes supernatural thrillers under the pseudonym Janell. In addition to writing, A'ndrea is a college professor and the president of Divine Garden Press, an independent publishing company based in Georgia. For more information, please visit her at www.andreawilsononline.com or www.wife101.com